THE
Mouse
AND THE
Elephant

A TALE FROM TURKEY

adapted by Cheyenne Cisco
illustrated by Cyd Moore

HOUGHTON MIFFLIN COMPANY
BOSTON
ATLANTA   DALLAS   GENEVA, ILLINOIS   PALO ALTO   PRINCETON

Once there was a mouse who liked
to show off.
"I'm the best!" he said. "I'm
Number 1! I'm the boss of this forest!"

"Watch out, Mouse," said his uncle.
"Don't let the elephant hear you say that.
 He is the real boss of the forest.
 He may get mad."

"I'll show that old elephant,"
said the mouse.
"Where is he? Where is he?
I'll break him into bits."

And the mouse set off to find the elephant.

The mouse walked and walked until
he saw a lizard.
"Hey, you!" said the mouse.
"Are you the elephant?"
"Me?" said the lizard.
"Oh, no. I'm just a lizard."

"Well, you are a lucky lizard then,"
said the mouse.
"Do you know why? If you were
the elephant, I'd break you into bits."
And the mouse kept walking.

The mouse walked and walked
until he saw a duck.
"Hey, you!" said the mouse.
"Are you the elephant?"
"Me?" said the duck.
"Oh, no. I'm just a duck."

"Well, you are a lucky duck then,"
said the mouse.
"Do you know why? If you were
the elephant, I'd break you into bits."
And the mouse kept walking.

The mouse walked and walked until
he saw a fox.
"Hey, you!" said the mouse.
"Are you the elephant?"
"Me?" said the fox.
"Oh, no. I'm just a fox."

"Well, you are a lucky fox then,"
  said the mouse.
"Do you know why? If you were
  the elephant, I'd break you into bits."
And the mouse kept walking.

The mouse walked and walked until
he saw an animal taking a bath.
It looked like a big, gray mountain.
It was the elephant!

"Hey, you!" said the mouse. "Are you the elephant? I came to tell you something. I'm the boss of this forest, so there! What do you think of that?"

13

The elephant pointed his trunk
at the tiny little mouse.
W H O O S H!
Out came all his bath water.

The mouse rolled over and over
and over.
The water carried him all the way
back home.

"That was a very lucky elephant,"
said the mouse.
"That big rain saved him. I was
going to break him into bits."

"Have a towel," said his uncle.